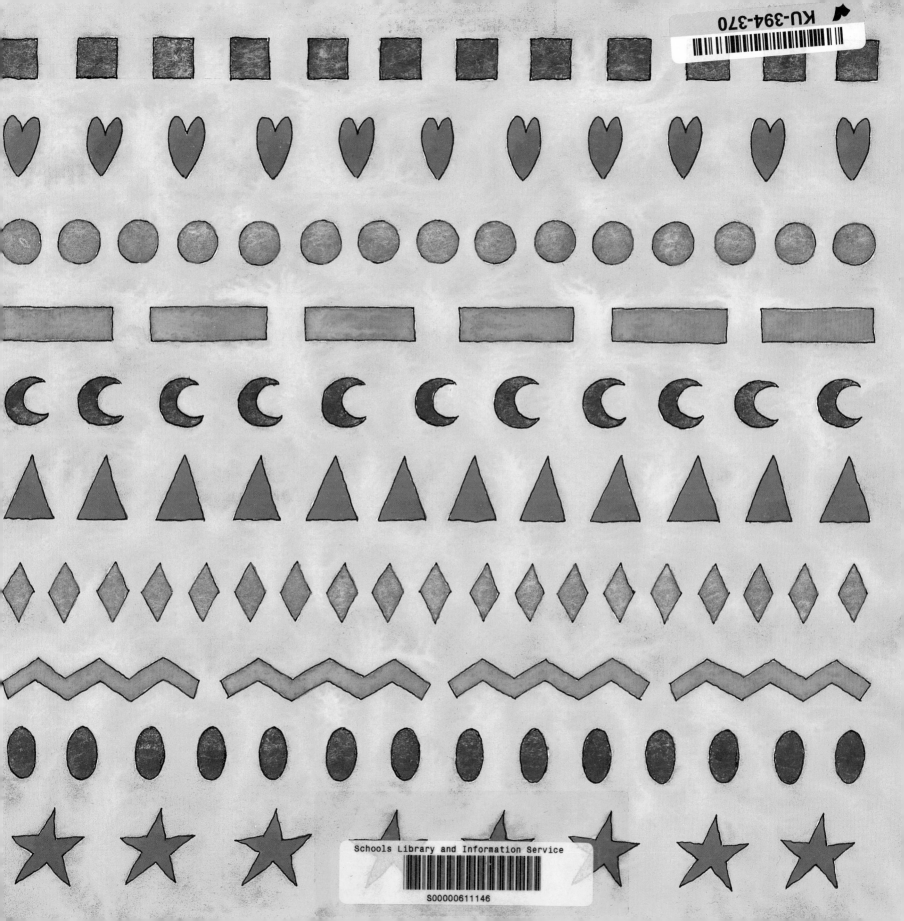

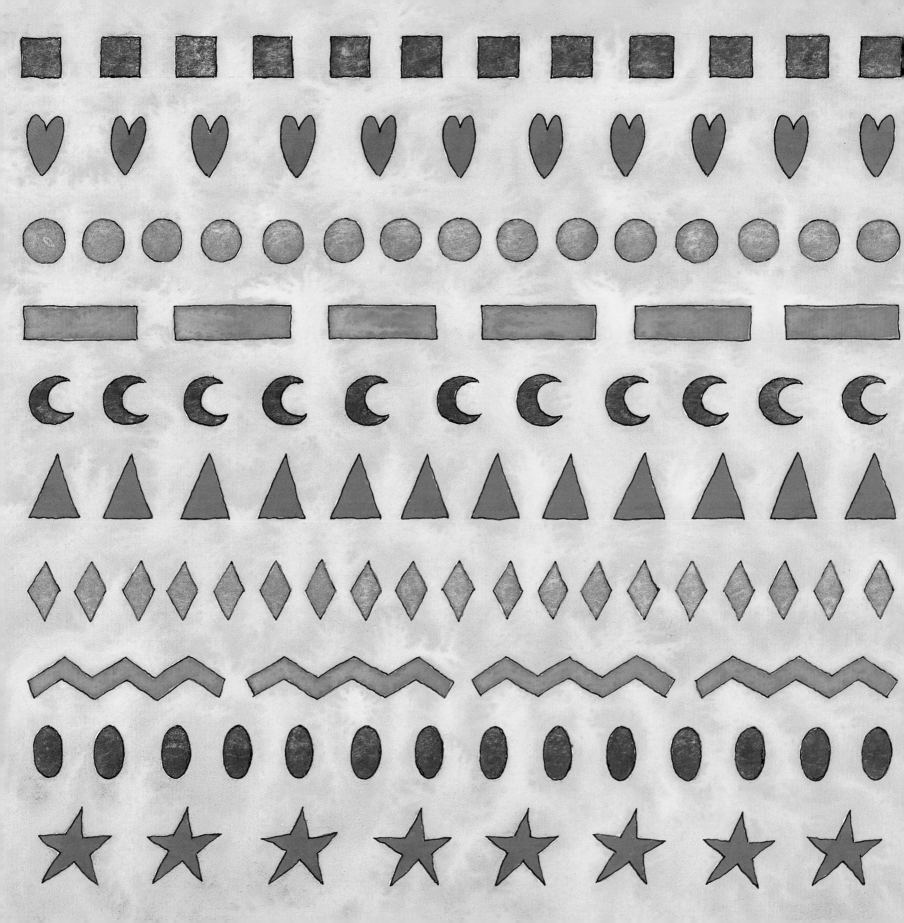

BEAR IN A SQUARE

Written by Stella Blackstone
Illustrated by Debbie Harter

BAREFOOT BOOKS

BATH

Find the bear
in the square

Find the hearts
in the queen's hair

Find the circles in the pool

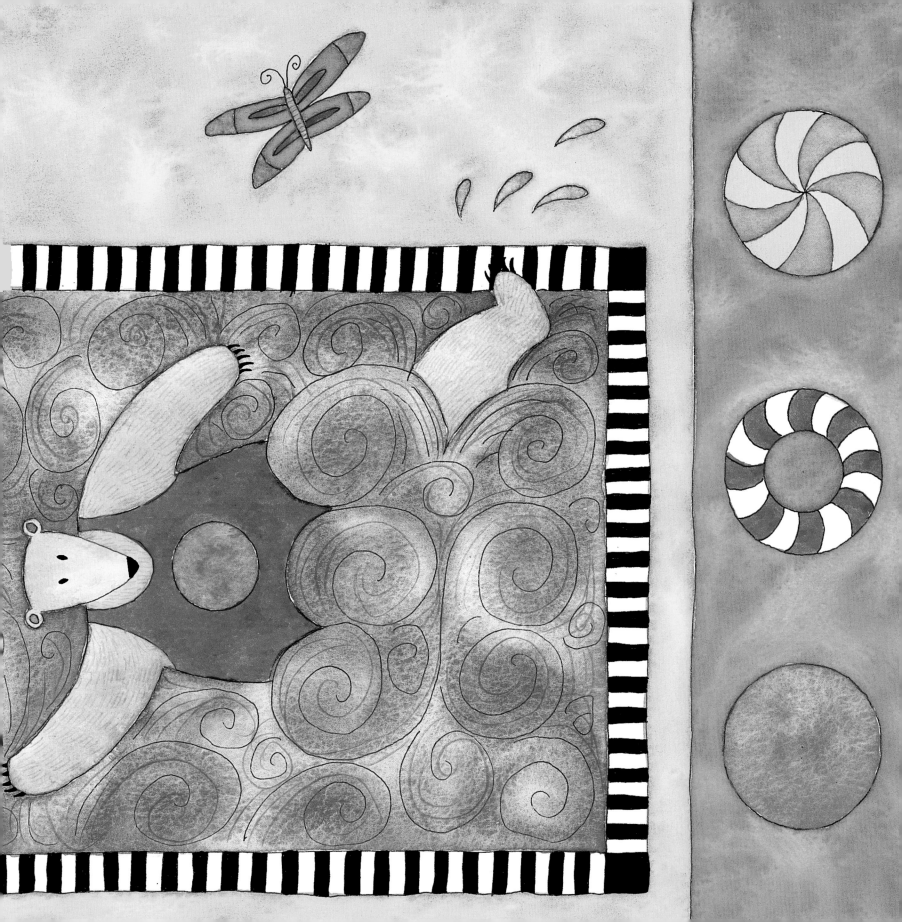

Find the rectangles in the school

Find the moons in the cave

Find the triangles on the wave

Find the diamonds on the crown

Find the zigzags around the clown

Find the ovals
in the park

Find the stars
in the dark

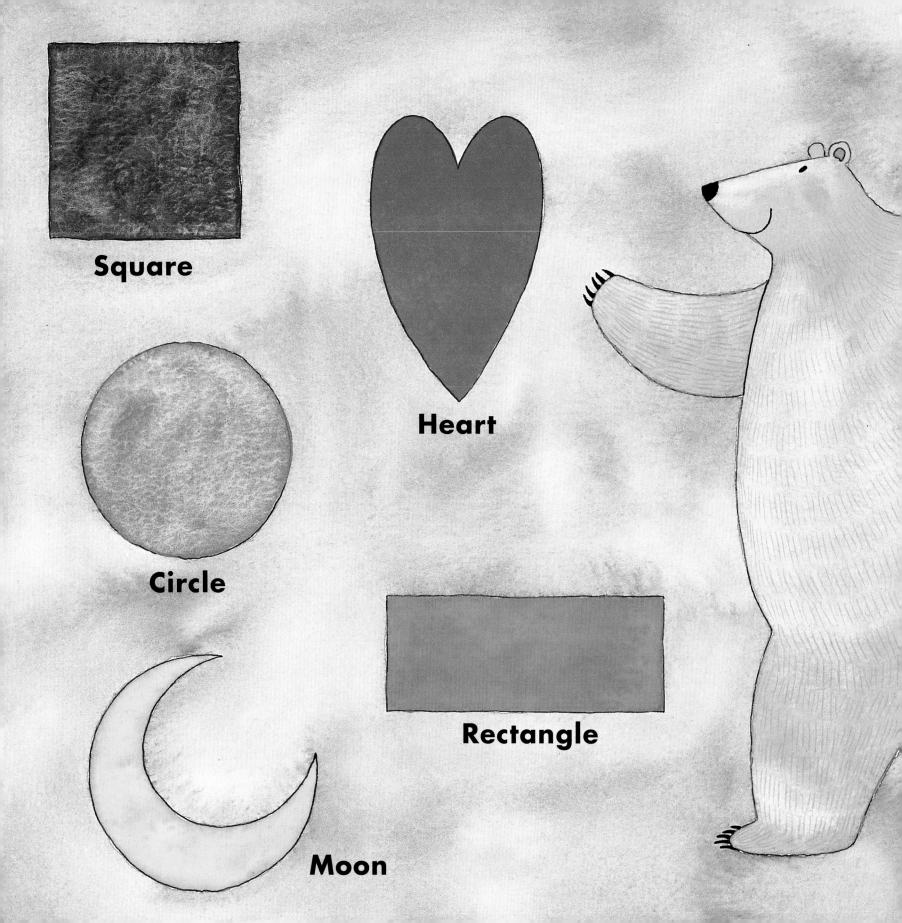

Square

Heart

Circle

Rectangle

Moon

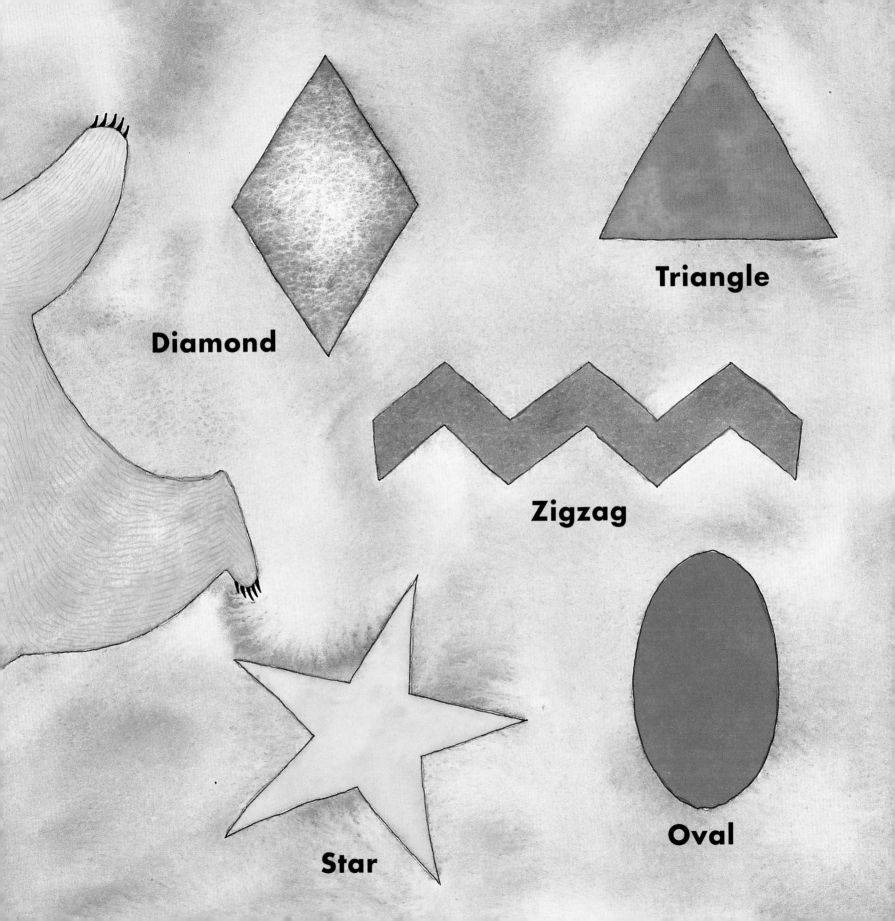

Diamond

Triangle

Zigzag

Star

Oval

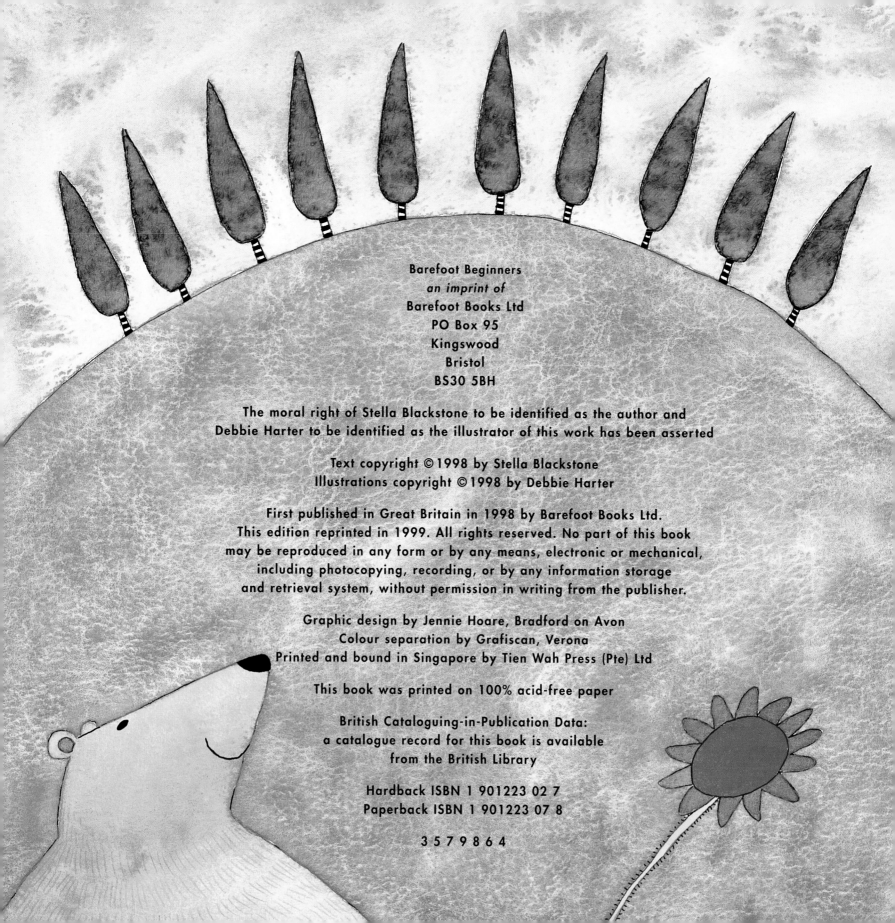

Barefoot Beginners
an imprint of
Barefoot Books Ltd
PO Box 95
Kingswood
Bristol
BS30 5BH

Graphic design by Jennie Hoare, Bradford on Avon
Colour separation by Grafiscan, Verona
Printed and bound in Singapore by Tien Wah Press (Pte) Ltd

This book was printed on 100% acid-free paper

British Cataloguing-in-Publication Data:
a catalogue record for this book is available
from the British Library

Hardback ISBN 1 901223 02 7
Paperback ISBN 1 901223 07 8

3 5 7 9 8 6 4

BAREFOOT BOOKS publishes high-quality picture books for
children of all ages and specialises in the work of artists and writers from
many cultures. If you have enjoyed this book and would like to receive a copy of
our current catalogue, please contact our London office – tel: 0171 704 6492
fax: 0171 359 5798 email: sales@barefoot-books.com
website: www.barefoot-books.com